HEAL THY WOMAN

EPISODE 1
"BLOOD ON THE GROUND"

WRITTEN BY:
KENYON R. DUDLEY

DIRECTED BY:
GOD

DUDLEY MEDIA GROUP
DUDLEY PUBLISHING HOUSE

PRODUCTION DRAFT: DECEMBER 27, 2013

FULL BLUE DRAFT: MARCH 26, 2021

PREP DATES:
SHOOT DATES:

Published by Dudley Publishing House (DP House)
McDonough, Georgia, 30252
www.dudleypublishinghouse.net

ISBN-13: 978-1-7365810-5-6

Cover Design by DP House | Media & Marketing Division
Printed in the United States of America

For book orders, author appearance inquires and interviews,
contact author's team at:

www.kenyondudley.com/contact

Dedication

I dedicate this book to multiple generations of women that's represented in my life.

First, I dedicate this to the love of my life, Jasmine B. Dudley. Watching your journey of healing up close has encouraged me to release this letter of healing to women around the world.

Secondly, I dedicate this to my Mother, Sharon Dudley. It was because of you and what I saw you have to live through that gave me such a heart and compassion for women.

Lastly, I dedicate this book to my baby girl and daughter Ms. Reagan Kimora Dudley. May you never have to know the trauma that the women who

came before you had to endure. But may you always

be aware of it and honor women from all walks of

life. May you never underestimate the level of

strength and endurance it takes to be a woman. May

you never underestimate your strength found in

God. May you remember always that you are

powerful, beautiful, wanted, valued, and loved first

by God, then Daddy, Mommy, and your family, but

most of all by yourself.

Content

Forward

I am woman.

I would often open my mouth to *hear me roar*, but I guess it's safe to say the cats of life can catch my tongue. Biologically, I'm defined as female; woman. But what exactly qualifies me to be a woman? Is it just biology or is it something more? Many of us go from womb to womanhood without much explanation as to what qualifies us as such in between those stages. As a consequence, we find ourselves in a whirlwind of issues, traumas, pains, and disappointments before we find out who we really are. Some of us are born into wholeness, while there are a lot of us that have to crawl our way to find it.

I'm reminded of the Samaritan woman in the John 4:1-42. She had no name in the bible, but her story is regarded to be one of the longest one-on-one encounters with Jesus. She didn't come limping; she didn't come bowed over. She didn't even come intentionally with a need as many in the scriptures did. She just walked through life, but she was unaware of her internal condition. The places that needed healing was not a visible wound like many Jesus had encountered during His ministry. At first glance, you couldn't tell she was in pain. But she had five previous husbands, and was currently living with a man that was not married to her. This tells me that *sistergirl* had some experience with a broken heart; maybe even feelings of abandonment, rejection, and unworthiness. *Fun fact!* Women during that time went to the well to draw water in groups. The fact that this woman went to get water alone most likely alludes to the fact that maybe she didn't fit into any social circle or girl groups. I just can imagine the pain of seeing everyone with their *bestie* or *girlfriends*, and not having the security of solid friendships. Not to mention the question of where was her mother? Did she have any blood sisters or aunts to go to? The Bible doesn't say.

She was just another woman from the womb that stumbled into womanhood. She—like me and maybe even like you—had an identity that was unknown. She—like me and maybe even like you—had it all together on the outside, but was damaged, broken, and lost on the inside. She—like me and maybe even like you—had an inner girl and an inner woman warring with one another on the inside trying to fight for power, position, and their place in the world.

Heal Thy Woman is an open invitation to *Heal Your Woman*. When we begin to heal our inner woman, we can rescue the inner little girl and let her know that she is safe to become all that God has designed her to become. When we *heal thy woman*, we can heal our world. As you journey through each book in this series you will identify with you, me and her. Together, we will heal her. Together, we will *Heal Thy Woman*.

Jasmine Dudley
Pastor, Author,
CEO of Naomi's Connect Technology,
Co-Founder of Dudley Publishing House.
www.jasminedudley.com

HEAL THY WOMAN

SETTING UP THE SCENE

WRITTEN BY:
KENYON R. DUDLEY

DIRECTED BY:
GOD

DUDLEY MEDIA GROUP
DUDLEY PUBLISHING HOUSE

PRODUCTION DRAFT: DECEMBER 27, 2013

FULL BLUE DRAFT: MARCH 26, 2021

PREP DATES:
SHOOT DATES:

Setting Up The Scene

She walks down the sidewalk with her red bottom stiletto pumps on, the latest purse hanging from her wrist, hair done, nails on point, and she drips. She walks into a restaurant to have lunch with her friends. She laughs, have a couple of sips of Stella, all while answering back her texts and emails right from her phone. She's a boss in her world. She seems to have it all under control. Even still; she drips. The red fluid runs from underneath her black leather skirt down her legs onto the seat where she's sitting and ultimately to the floor. She's dripping and no one seems to notice. Moreover, no one seems to care.

She pays for the check and closes out lunch with her girlfriends, proceeds to leave the restaurant and walk back down the sidewalk to her black Mercedes. The valet drives her car up and opens the door for her. She tips, yet drips. The young valet notices, but is too afraid to say what he sees. He closes the door, "Have a great day ma'am," and watches as her car pulls away from the pool of red that came from her, yet *he* now stands in.

Everywhere she goes, she flows. She leaves a pool of blood on the floor. It's messy. It's red. It smells. It is an issue running right from the private places of her heart, staining her life with secret depression and despair.

Yeah, she leaves a pool of blood on the ground where she walks. Yet, no one dares to tell her. In fact, no one *has* to. For she already knows about the problem that flows from her design and make-up. But, that's just it. She uses the make-up to try to mask the truth of the matter. She has enveloped herself in the lifestyle of body contouring, and BBS is next on her agenda; but everywhere she goes, she drips with the *real* issue. It runs out of her, *oozes* out of her. The issue is so *bad* not even the life source itself seems to want to stay connected to her. Something is wrong. Something is dead. Something smells and it is *not* a feminine hygiene problem, as you would suppose. Her life is lifeless and closed. She walks around as if she is happy, but she *ain't* happy. Her ex knows it. Her children feel it. Her pastor discerns it. Moreover, all of her girlfriends can see it. She is *dying* a silent, slow, and painful death and she needs a healing touch.

The rape, the past abuse, the trauma, the being married to lies, the teenage sexual escapades with her old friend that nobody knows about, the negative voices in her mind, even the religiosity she's learned from Big Mamma all collide bringing her to this place of hemorrhaging. She's bleeding while living; and while it seems no one cares, what's more is she has lost care for herself.

Nevertheless, there is one thing that is keeping her alive even though she has lost so much blood. It is her small inkling of a belief in God. That small piece of hope that she has left in a Savior that Big Momma once taught her about. Her hope—that God can and will heal—her is what keeps her going. Her Big Momma's ideology that He is the only man who consistently loves her even in the toughest times is what she leans on. That is the hope that keeps her even on the days when she does not even want to be kept.

While it is right to believe that God is a healer and the lover of your soul, my Sister, you must understand that He will only heal those who bring their broken pieces to Him. And His love is only worth-while when you receive Him. It is not enough *just* to believe, but like the woman with the issue of blood, you have to walk—*crawl if you have to*—toward your promise of freedom, healing, and toward God's love. And not only do you have to walk toward it; but you must allow it to embrace

19

you; permeating down to the deepest darkest most intimate parts of you; if you're going to be completely healed. *Woman*, I think it's high time you realize that Jesus is passing by. Your healing is just up the way. However, it is imperative that you find the drive, the seek, the hunger to push beyond your tiredness, your apathy, your disappointment, and your pain. You have to get to the *One* who can heal you best at any cost. Face it. You have tried everything else. You have tried every*one* else. The depression you are fighting, the remorse you feel, the guilt you are hanging on to, the dirtiness you live with every day, the disappointment you hold in your heart even while you work; yeah, God can heal. But, it is up to you to search for Him, reach for Him, and go beyond your normal routine. Be willing to go another route, do something out of your norm. Be willing to scrape and scuffle to your healing if you have to. But at all cost, be willing to open up to another man who isn't man at all. He's divinity. And He's your healing balm.

There is a man who cares. Moreover, not only does He care, but also He wants to see about you and your brokenness. Unbelievably, you *were* His woman first. He made you, and you are His. I know you're broken right now. Torn up about some things happening in your life right now. But your maker, the first lover of your soul wants to mend you back together again. And He seeks to restore you and make you whole; bringing you back into your rightful position with Him. I know you haven't felt a reassuring reaffirming touch in a *long* time. He wants to touch you in places and ways that no man, no woman, no alcohol, no sex toy, no career, no money, or any earthly tangible thing could ever do.

You just have to make up in your mind that you are going to be honest. You are going to have to face *that* issue head on. The issue of blood. Acknowledge that you are bleeding. Acknowledge that the drip is out of control, and that you need something that is beyond human comprehension and ability to stop the hemorrhaging. Acknowledge that you need God on this one.

Such is the reality that the women in *Heal Thy Woman* have had to face at this juncture of their life. Follow their story as they face some of the things that you face even now. Walk with them. Talk with them through the pages. Imagine that you are in the room sitting next to them. Take time to help them move into their freedom, and their stories help you move into yours. My mother always said, "What you make happen for others God will make happen for you." As you flip through the pages of their lives, hear their hearts. Hear their voices. Hear their trauma; and hear their pain. *Walk with them,* why don't you? *Understand* them. Relate, and then help them as they help you. How do I help them, you might ask? The best way to help anyone is to see yourself first. Relate to their stories. Then see your girlfriend, your mother, your sister, or some other familiar woman in the stories of these women. Empathize with them. And as you empathize, make a choice to offer this prayer up on behalf of the women in these pages, the women in your life, and even for yourself, *"Lord, heal thy woman."* It is a prayer that I pray each and every day for the women in my life, recognizing that if they are not healed then nothing and *no one* in the house is. In fact, no one in the bloodline is. The new life starts in the womb, and it is the woman who carries that life. If she is whole, then so are the many generations and nations birthed from her. If she is not, then neither are they that come from her.

Sistah, are you ready to heal? Are you ready to become new, revived, refreshed, and renewed? If you are, then allow me to introduce you to your new friends whom you will walk this journey of healing alongside. Turn the page and meet the ladies who will be in your birthing room. They'll serve as your midwives and help you clean the blood up from the ground of your life.

HEAL THY WOMAN

MEET THE CHARACTERS:
"CHARACTER BREAKDOWN"

WRITTEN BY:
KENYON R. DUDLEY

DIRECTED BY:
GOD

DUDLEY MEDIA GROUP
DUDLEY PUBLISHING HOUSE

PRODUCTION DRAFT: DECEMBER 27, 2013

FULL BLUE DRAFT: MARCH 26, 2021

PREP DATES:
SHOOT DATES:

MAIN CHARACTERS

- **LAUREN CASSIDY.** The young woman who's trapped in a romantic infidelity. She's married to Mel Cassidy who will be introduced next. She is a 23-year-old African American college graduate who used to be the cream of the crop in school. Always known as the class clown in high school. *That is* until she had a baby out of wedlock. She then got pregnant for a second time by the same guy. He eventually married her because of family pressure. They were super young when they got married. Though she earned her Bachelors in post-secondary education and currently lives as an 11th grade math teacher; she's still not totally happy with herself or her marriage. Wanting so badly to be grown and to have her own say in her life, she moved out of her parents' house at an early age and married who she thought was the man of her dreams.

- **MEL CASSIDY** is a young 24-year-old African American man and a college drop out. He is a rich ritzy boy who comes from a very well to do family, but his father left the home while he was in college. This provoked him to become a college dropout. He met Lauren in his sophomore year of university, got her pregnant twice, and was forced to marry her. He never got a chance to experience his entire college life so instead of taking care of his family he still wants to party. He can't keep a job since he dropped out of college. All he does is work on cars at home. You would never know that he is from a rich family. His family has nothing to do with him since he made the decision to throw his career and dreams away to marry Lauren. As far as they were concerned, she wasn't good enough for him. He is most certainly not in love with Lauren. He's a big time adulterer. He's even slept with some of Lauren's family members and friends, but what he doesn't know is that he's forced Lauren to step out on him a couple of times as well as she has sought revenge for the hurt he has caused her.

- Then there is **TONI LARK.** Toni is a beautiful light-skinned 34-year-old woman who can be nothing but drama at times. She is bi-racial, and has episodes where she's trying to balance her identity between both cultures. She's of African American and Asian descent. She has been officially diagnosed with bipolar disorder, but her family keeps it undercover. She's a well-known Atlanta based writer and drama teacher at Morris Dave High School. She has a P.H.D. in Theatre (Performance) and she is the founder of her own non-profit performing arts center. She is all about teaching the next generation of actors and creatives so that the life of theatre, arts, and entertainment can live on. Toni is married to

Sean Lark who will be introduced next and together they are able to afford a *huge* house on the lake in North Georgia. Toni has been the *ride-or-die* chick for Sean ever since middle school. They were high school sweet hearts. Make no mistake about it, she is from the ghetto. The streets of University Avenue near downtown Atlanta to be exact. She was just blessed enough to have a talent which afforded her a come-up. She had an alcoholic as a father and her mother ran out on them for another man while she was just a freshman in high school. She is the oldest of her siblings. After almost fifteen years of marriage, Sean decides to step out on her provoking an all-out war in her home. She eventually steps out on him too; and when she does Sean can't handle it. The drama erupts from there.

- **SEAN LARK** is a 35-year-old African American man. He is a construction worker by day and a drug dealer by night. After years of arguing with his wife about stopping the drug-dealing game Sean decides to take all sorts of higher education classes to become everything under the sun. His main goal? Always make money. But he also wanted to honor his word to his wife by not running the streets anymore. He has taken classes to be a plumber. He's taken classes to receive his CDL license. He has even tried to become a realtor, and a catalog salesperson, but has never completed *any* of the courses. As a kid, he saw his father beat his mother a lot so he never knew how to really love or be loved by a woman. This caused him to turn to the streets as a young teenager in the first place. When Toni met him in middle school he was already a bonefide drug dealer, but she thought she could change him.

- Meet **LISA JONES.** She deals with the conflicted romantic & commemorative infidelity issue. Now, Lisa is kind of the odd ball that has been trained to fit in with the group. She is a 29-year-old Caucasian woman who has been adopted into the family through Sean's sister Angela. We'll get to Angela in just a second. Lisa never really knew her biological parents. Her sexually abusive uncle raised her. One day her car caught on fire while she and her 3-month-old baby, who is the seed of her uncle, were in it. She managed to escape out of the car with the baby. Nevertheless, she was stranded on the highway when Angela and her husband Brent just so happened to see her while driving up the road to a revival at the church. From there they unofficially adopted her into their family. A few years after her adoption, she married Dillan while still in her 20's, and had four more kids by him. She always aspired to be a lawyer, but never got a chance to go back to school. She has not been happy since their marriage.

- **DILLAN JONES** is the hardworking construction worker who works with the same construction company as Sean does. He is the faithful 31-year-old husband to Lisa. He's African American and he loves his wife and kids. He tries his best to take care of his family, but he is a bit of a *late-bloomer*. He's just a little behind the rest according to what culture says. He is naïve to the fact that his wife has fallen out of love with him, is a serial cheater, and does not want to be married to him anymore.

- **ANGELA RASHAUD.** Angela's husband is committing opportunistic infidelity, and soon she will have to face her own opportunity to cross the line. She is the preacher of the family. She's 53-years-old.

A very eccentric and spiritual individual.

Every word that comes out of her mouth is

about God. She is a bit of a fanatic in some

people's eyes, but what many don't know is

that she has to be. Her walk with God keeps

her sane. In our story, Angela currently

serves as the Associate Pastor of a small-

town church in Rex, Georgia. She's actually

the first female pastor *ever* in the town. This

causes her a bit of grief from the town folks.

She doesn't get much respect from the

Senior Pastor that she serves under because

he's a classic male-chauvinist. He doesn't

even want her on his staff, but she was

already voted in by her late father who was

the previous Bishop of the church before he

passed. The current pastor has tried to seduce Angela multiple times wanting her to sleep with him for continued favor in the church, but her faith is too strong.

- **BRENT RASHAUD** is Angela's husband. He is a 60-year-old African American man who is a major realtor around town. He is a shrewd businessman. He's had affairs with plenty of women in the past, but there's one particular affair that takes the cake. Causing his preacher-wife to lose her cool, terribly.

- **KERRY LOCKLEAR** is the 33-year-old bi-racial sister of Toni. She was raised with the same upbringing as Toni had. She looks up to her big sister, and has followed her everywhere she went in life. If Toni moved to a particular state, so would Kerry. If Toni dated a guy back in high school, then Kerry would try to date someone close to the guy if she couldn't convince Toni's man to cheat with her. If Toni jumped off a cliff, Kerry might've too. Everything Toni does Kerry does, and she desires for her husband to be *just* like who she thinks her brother-in-law Sean is: handsome, charismatic, fly, outgoing, and a *showstopper*. Like her sister, Toni, Kerry has been with her husband since they were teenagers. She never got a chance to experience life either. She has been married to Chris for exactly 10 years. For the first few years of their marriage, it was *hell* for Kerry. Chris would beat her to a pulp. Now-a-days he's slacked up on the domestic violence, but he still checks her every now and then with his fist. Their marriage eventually come to a boiling point when Kerry has had enough and seeks revenge.

- Lastly, there is **CHRIS LOCKLEAR.** He is a 34-year-old African American plumber. He is an alcoholic who is not satisfied with his life at all. He has two kids with Kerry. He can only afford for them to live in a house on the eastside of the ghetto. Let's just say he's a ticking time bomb waiting to explode.

You're invited into these ladies' world full of rejection, hatred, cheating, lies, deceit, hurt, and healing. They're a family of women who carry generational hurt and pain. The scars and wounds acquired by each woman paint the picture of the vast array of women in the world who are suffering from their own trauma and pain. This family of women are the epitome of what happens when some men can't or refuse to stand up and cover their homes. They can't because of their own hurts and hang-ups. These women, your new girlfirends, are the epitome of what happens when generational baggage has not been checked at the foot of Jesus. They are the greatest example I can give at the moment when *the issue of blood* hasn't met a man named Jesus. They are the example of what women fall into when led astray by their own enticement.

They are the epitome of what every single woman knows in her heart when she lies down in the cold sheets of her bed alone, body yearning for someone to love her and not take advantage of her hips, lips, or fingertips. Moreover, they are the essence of what it looks like to find hope in the middle of the wildest of storms. Here is a story all about how women deal with their wounds. Some heal faster than others. Some never heal at all. But all of them have the same opportunity to lay their burdens down at the feet of a man who with one touch can cure them all. These women are real. Their stories are real. Because they are the stories of the one who reads this book. They are the stories of Grandma who died with her secrets buried in her heart. They are the stories of Auntie who has to have a sip of wine at the end of each day just to calm her nerves.

What she's seeking in the bottle may very well not be peace and calm from the day at all. But she may be seeking wholeness from the broken pieces of her fragmented heart. These are the stories your Mother yearns to tell you she went through too, but because of the fear of condemnation she's learned to hold it in too. Take this opportunity to see the other woman through the lenses of your own experiences, and relate to her. Then pray for her the same prayer I'm praying for you my friend, *"Lord, heal thy woman."* For every woman needs a girlfriend truly praying for her and a strong male presence who don't mind doing the same. Let's enter into the lives of the women I've just introduced to you. Over the course of a book series, like an episodic show on television, I will unpack and unfold the lives of these women so that you can see God's plan to heal women everywhere. Let's follow their journey to

healing and wholeness.

HEAL THY WOMAN

EPISODE 1:
BLOOD ON THE GROUND

WRITTEN BY:
KENYON R. DUDLEY

DIRECTED BY:
GOD

DUDLEY MEDIA GROUP
DUDLEY PUBLISHING HOUSE

PRODUCTION DRAFT: DECEMBER 27, 2013

FULL BLUE DRAFT: MARCH 26, 2021

PREP DATES:
SHOOT DATES:

TEASER

Screen is pitch black.

The title, Heal Thy Woman, appears, in red cursive letters, in the middle of the blackness on the screen. Then it slowly fades away as the next scene appears.

EXTERIOR: Nighttime. 8 PM.

In this first scene, you see the front outside view of Lauren and Mel Cassidy's middle class townhouse. In the driveway, you see a raggedy piece of junk that is supposed to be a car that Mel is working on. You also see a red Chevy Impala that belongs to Mel, and an old white beat up Honda accord that belongs to Lauren. The flowerbed lights, around the shrubs close to the front black door, are on. One

light is broken from the kids playing around in the

front yard. All of the lights are on in the house. You

can tell by seeing every window lit up with light.

The street they live on is silent at the moment.

INTERIOR: Inside Mel and Lauren's bedroom.
Still nighttime. 8:03 PM.

Cut to a wide view of Lauren laying on the unmade

up bed, in her dim lit room. She is laughing and

talking loudly on the cell phone while her husband,

Mel is in the shower in the master bathroom.

You can hear the shower water running in the

background.

She speaks.

LAUREN *(excited)*

(Laughing loudly) Giiiiirrrl, I know! I know! *(beat)* Mmmm humm, I can't wait to get away from these darn kids. You best believe I'm gone get my drink on tonight at the club!

She *BEATS* then laughs even louder as if the person on the phone has just said the funniest joke in the world. She's so overwhelmed by what was said that she's nearly on the floor from laughter.

LAUREN *(now nearly choking)*

Girl I'm telln' you! I'mma *(singing)* 'blame it on the *a-a-a-a-a-al-co-hol!*'

She screams to the top of her lungs laughing.

CUT TO:

INTERIOR: Inside of Lisa's bedroom.

Nighttime. 8:15 PM.

You see a close up view of Lisa putting on her red stilettos. She is sitting on the edge of her unmade up bed in her dim lit room talking on her house phone to Lauren.

LISA *(smiling)*

Lauren you crazy girl, but I know what you mean! Girl I'm bout to try to dance on every fine piece of sexy chocolate I see tonight!

She laughs.

CUT TO:

*Lauren's bedroom. She continues to lay across the
bed.*

LAUREN

Lisa you a gangsta fa' real. How in the world is you
gone be dancn' up on all these men and yo husband
comin' wit us?

CUT TO:

*Lisa standing in front of her mirror on her dresser.
She's putting on red lip gloss.*

LISA *(disgusted)*

Ooo, girl he slow as hel--. Uhn uh. Nope. I'm not
even going there. *(Beat)* Now Lauren you know he
ain't gone do nothn.' Girl, all he gone do is sit there

in a seat all night and smile. Shhh…weak. That's all that fool ever does is smile. He ain't gone dance, and he darn sho' ain't gone step to no man that I'm dancn' with! *(laughing)* He too scared…child and weak.

LAUREN *(voice-over)*

(laughing) Lisa, girl, you know you wrong. Mmm mmm you so wrong.

Lisa takes a BEAT. She stops making her face up and rolls her eyes while still looking at herself in the mirror. She takes a deep breath of frustration.

LISA

Honey, *I AM NOT WRONG!* What's wrong is that sad excuse for a man in there still think I'm in love with his sorry...

While Lauren talks, Lisa is reacting in disbelief. She cuts Lisa off.

LAUREN *(voice-over)*

But Lisa, Dillan is a good man. He works. He loves you and all them doggone kids. Shoot girl, he even come home to cook *AND* clean the house. *AFTER* he gets off work. *Giiiirrrl, I WISH* I had a man to cook around this house, or at least pick up his own dirty drawls.

CUT TO:

Cut to Lauren still sitting in the bed.

While Lisa talks, Lauren is reacting.

LISA *(voice-over)*

(disgusted) See, that's what I'm talkn' about. He just so weak. He does whatever I say. Whenever I say it. I need somebody strong, who can hold their own. You know? Tell me what to do every once in a while!

LAUREN

Well I guess you right. *(beat)* Dillan *IS* kind of weak. *(smiling with sarcasm)* I mean you can tell that fool to go jump off a building right now and he'd go do it.

The two share a short laugh. It's cut off by Mel's voice.

CUT TO:

Cut to Mel standing in the bathroom doorway with every piece of clothing on, but his shirt. He walks over to the closet and grabs a shirt and cardigan.

He speaks.

MEL *(upset)*

Dang Lauren you still on that phone? We gotta go! Tell that gossipn' Lisa to get off the doggone phone and get dressed. Everybody waitn' on us at the club. Yo uncle Sean just called me askn' where we at!?

LAUREN *(disgusted)*

Stop fussin' Mel and shut up. Ain't nobody even

talkn' to you.

CUT TO:

Cut to a backside view of Lisa walking out of her

room, down her toy-infested hallway, to her front

door while Lauren and Mel argue through the

phone.

LISA

Tell dat boy to shut up and calm down. Beauty

takes time.

Lauren and Mel stop arguing, and Lauren begins to

speak to Lisa again through the phone.

LAUREN *(voice-over)*

Girl *(beat)* let me get off this phone and get dressed before me and this boy have it out. *(beat)* Mel get yo lil daughter.

LISA

(laughing) Ok girl. I'll see y'all at the spot. *(beat)* All right, later.

LAUREN *(voice-over)*

Lil girl if you don't stop *JUMPIN'* on this bed, I'm gone tear yo behind up!

Phone hangs up.

CUT TO:

You see a wide view of Lisa's entire living room that is dirty and filled with the kids' toys. She stands at the front door as she hangs up the house phone. The phone hook is on the small table right next to the front door. She looks around for Dillan. He's nowhere to be found.

LISA *(yelling)*

Dillan!? DILLAN!?

Dillan stumbles into the living room, from the kitchen. He can be a clumsy guy. Always nervously laughing. He has a turkey sandwich in his hand. His mouth is packed with half of it.

DILLAN

Lisa!? *(beat)* Lisa you ready baby?

LISA *(disgusted)*

That's what the heck I've been calln' you for. I've been calln' you for the past twenty minutes! C'mon here! We late! Daddy and everybody else are waitin' on us at the place!

EXTERIOR: In front of Lisa and Dillan's house. Nighttime. 8:35 PM.

She opens the front door and leaves him hurriedly following her to the car. Lisa continues to fuss at Dillan. The disrespect is real.

LISA *(upset)*

You got me all late and stuff…

Lisa stands at the passenger door waiting for Dillan to let her in the car.

Dillan struggles with getting himself together. He nervously situates his sandwich so that he can get the car keys out of his pocket and unlock the doors. He is taking a long time and Lisa's getting more and more frustrated.

LISA *(...cont.)*

Come on fool and let me in…

She stumps her feet and breaks the heel of her stiletto. Dillan isn't opening the car door fast enough. Now she's pissed.

LISA

Darmit! *(grabs broken shoe)* Look what you done made me do now. I done broke my darn shoe. *(beat)* You bastard! *(beat)* Hurry up and let me in this car…

She continues to fuss as the Intro Credits of the show rolls.

FADE OUT:

Fade in the Intro Credits and music.

SCENE ONE:

FADE IN:

EXTERIOR: Outside of the nightclub, *Spirits*. It is nighttime. 9 PM.

You see a panoramic view of the club. Multiple colored lights around the building. From the sky, you see a long line of people waiting to get into the popular Atlanta nightclub.

The camera pans down and around the front of the club where you see a close up view of the people in line. They are standing behind a red rope, and they are so anxious and excited to get in to party that some are dancing in line.

CUT TO:

You see a wide shot of two big buff bouncers at the front door who are dressed in all black suits. One of them is African American while the other is Caucasian. The African American bouncer has on black shades. He has a clipboard with the list of names of VIP members, and the Caucasian bouncer is checking for ID to admit the regular customers. They both have guns, walkie-talkies, and earpieces on their person.

While all of this is taking place, you hear the loud music, in the club, bumping. In addition, you hear the crowd shouting and roaring on the dance floor. It's live and lit to say the least.

CUT TO:

Cut to a close up of the club marquee. It says, in florescent purple and green lights, Spirits.

CUT TO:

You see a wide shot of Lisa and Dillan standing about midway in the line at the front of the club. Lisa is looking around. By now, she is frustrated, her patience has worn thin, and she is anxious to get in the club to get away from Dillan.

Dillan is standing behind her with a quirky look on his face.

Lisa speaks.

LISA *(frustrated)*

Ugh! What the heck are those bouncers doin' up there? *(beat) C'MON!*

Lisa's cell phone rings. She answers.

INTERIOR: Inside the nightclub. It is nighttime. 9:20 PM.

CUT TO:

Cut to close up of Lauren sitting at a table in the club, covering her other ear so that she can hear. You hear loud music in the background, and the club is live. People are jumping everywhere, walking around, talking loud, dancing on one another, and lights are flickering everywhere on the dance floor behind Lauren.

Lauren speaks.

LAUREN

Hello?! *(beat)* Lisa? Where you at girl? We're

waiting on you. We've been here for an hour now.

CUT TO:

Cut to close up of Lisa's frustrated face.

Lisa speaks.

LISA

Ugh! Lauren. *(beat)* Girl I'm stuck in this line at the

front tryin' to get in. I will be there.

You see Lisa's POV towards people in front of her,

the camera widens out.

LISA *(cont'd)*

ONCE THESE PEOPLE HURRY UP AND MOVE

OUT THE WAY!

The girls standing directly in front of her look back

at her with a nasty attitude. Then they turn back

around and ignore Lisa's rant.

CUT TO:

Cut back to close up of Lauren.

She speaks.

When she begins to speak, the camera pans out to a

wide view of everyone sitting at the table with her.

Kerry, Chris, Sean, Toni, Mel, and Brent are all

sitting at the table. Everyone is in his or her own world. Well, everybody except for Toni. She's listening in on the phone conversation.

LAUREN

What?! You stuck at the door? Wait a minute, hold up.

She covers the bottom of the phone to talk to Toni.

Toni looks at Lauren as if she is waiting for an answer.

TONI

What girl? What's up?

LAUREN *(laughing)*

Her crazy butt stuck at the front door in line!

TONI

Tell that girl to just jump the line and tell the

bouncers she's with Brent's VIP crew!

LAUREN

All right, hold on.

Lauren gets back on the phone with Lisa.

LAUREN *(...cont.)*

Lisa!? Toni said just skip everybody in line and tell

the bouncers you with Uncle Brent's crew.

CUT TO:

Cut to wide view of Lisa leaning on the wall. Her hair is completely messed up now. She's huffing and puffing, as if she has just been in a catfight.

Dillan is picking her shoes up from the ground.

Lisa snatches them out of his hand. He steps back. She begins to speak to Lauren as she struggles to put her heels back on.

LISA *(tired)*

Girl I done already tried that. Those fools just picked me up and threw me in the back of the line.

CUT TO:

Cut back to wide shot of everyone at the table.

LAUREN *(surprised)*

THEY WHAT?! Oh naw, wait a minute girl!

Now everyone at the table turns their attention to Lauren. They're startled by her reaction.

TONI *(anxious)*

What? What she say?

LAUREN

She said that they picked her up and threw her in the back of the line!

CUT TO:

Cut to close up of Brent standing over the table with a beer in his hand.

BRENT *(confused)*

Who is that?!

CUT TO:

Cut to two shot of Toni and Lauren. They respond simultaneously.

LAUREN & TONI *(sarcastic)*

Yo daughter.

CUT TO:

Cut back to close up of Brent.

BRENT

Lisa?! *(Beat)* It's always her. Where she at?

CUT TO:

Cut to close up of Lauren.

LAUREN

She up at the front in line. Uncle Brent go get yo

daughter before she been done caught a case out

there. They won't let her in cuz they don't think she

with us.

CUT TO:

Cut to wide shot of the table again.

BRENT

All right! I'll take care of it.

Brent walks off through the crowd toward the front door of the club.

LAUREN

Uncle Brent said he comin' up there right now.

(beat) All right?

Lauren hangs up her cell phone.

CUT TO:

Cut to wide view of Brent walking through the crowd. He finally reaches the front door.

CUT TO:

Cut to three shot of Brent and the two bouncers. Brent gives one of the bouncers a handshake.

BIG BLU

What it is patna?

BRENT

Nothing much baby! *(beat)* What's goin' on with y'all not letting my daughter in, man?

CUT TO:

Close up of Big Blu.

BIG BLU *(confused)*

Yo daughter? Lil Tia ain't came through here captain.

CUT TO:

Cut to wide shot of Brent with the club scene behind him.

BRENT *(sarcastic)*

Naw fool, I ain't talkn' bout Tiara. I'm talkn' bout my oldest daughter, Lisa. Now where is she?

Wide shot of Brent walking out the front door looking at the line.

From Brent's POV you see Lisa and Dillan way in the back of the line jumping up and down trying to get the attention of Brent.

LISA *(yelling)*

We back here daddy! Daddy! A, daddy!

DILLAN *(yelling)*

Yo Mr. B! Back here!

CUT TO:

Cut to mid shot of Brent and the two bouncers standing behind him.

BRENT

A, there they go!

Brent signals for them to come on up to the front of the line.

BRENT *(yelling)*

Yall c'mon!

BRADFORD

Sorry Mr. Rashaud. We didn't know they were with you.

Brent turns around and looks at the other bouncer. The camera pans to the side of them so their faces can be seen.

BRENT

Ha, it's okay this time Bradford. But, don't let this sh-- right here happen again. Ok? Next time I'm getting' C.C. on the phone.

Lisa and Dillan run into frame. They're both tired.

LISA

Hey daddy!

DILLAN

Hey Mr. B.

Brent turns around to them. The camera cuts the two bouncers out of frame and tightens in on a 3 mid shot of Lisa, Brent, and Dillan.

Brent and Lisa hug. Brent kissed Lisa on the cheek.

BRENT

Hey babygirl. What's happenin'?

Brent gives Dillan a handshake.

BRENT *(...cont.)*

What it is son-in-law? Y'all c'mon. I got us a table
in the VIP suite.

CUT TO:

*Cut to wide shot of everybody in the front of the
club.*

Brent turns around to lead them into the club. Lisa and Dillan follow.

Lisa licks her tongue at one of the bouncers, and she hits the other one on the back.

The one that she hits bucks at her as if he's going to get her. Lisa scrambles and runs behind Brent and Dillan.

Then the bouncers go back to checking names and ID.

FADE OUT:

Picture fades to black.

SCENE TWO:

FADE IN:

Picture fades back into scene.

You see a wide shot of Brent walking up the stairs

to the VIP suite while Lisa and Dillan follow him.

Lisa's fixing her hair and dress while Dillan is

helping her up the steps. She doesn't really want his

help.

By this time, Toni and Sean have already made their

way to the dance floor.

Brent, Lisa, and Dillan make their way to the table

and then Chris speaks.

Cut to a mid-shot of Chris sitting at the table. He is so drunk his eyes can hardly open.

CHRIS

What it is folk?!

CUT TO:

You see a wide shot of Lisa beginning to give a fake smile. She puts it on every time she gets around the family because she wants everyone to always think that everything is okay with her life. She's a cover girl for sure.

LISA

Heeeeyyyy!

The camera pans out to fit everyone in the scene.

Lisa goes around the table and hugs everyone starting with Lauren.

LISA

Hey girl! What's up Mel?! I heard you talkin' all that junk on the phone tonight. *Kerrryyyyy!* Hey girl! What it is boo?!

Dillan follows her around the table and silently hugs everyone until he gets to Kerry.

KERRY *(seductive)*

And, hey to you too Mr. Dillan!

CUT TO:

Cut to close up of Lisa looking at Dillan strangely, as she takes her seat next to Lauren.

CUT TO:

Cut to a three shot of Dillan standing, Kerry sitting, and Chris sitting next to her.

Dillan is so naïve that he falls right into the trap of Kerry's flirtatious salutation. He smiles and starts to laugh nervously.

DILLAN

Hey Kerry! What ya been up to?

KERRY *(seductive)*

Oh nothing much. It's yo world playa. I'm just a
squirrle tryn' to get a (she fondles with Dillan's
penis area for a quick second) *NUT.*

CUT TO:

Cut to wide shot of everyone at the table.

*Dillan is kind of startled. Lisa and Chris quickly
respond at the same time.*

LISA

All right now Dillan. Get yo gullible butt over here
for I have to catch a case.

Chris grabs Kerry's arm tightly

CHRIS

Man, Kerry I'll kill you.

Kerry snatches her arm away from Chris in

embarrassment and anger.

KERRY

Negro please. Don't you ever grab me like that.

Like you own me. I ain't Tina and you ain't Ike.

She's had one too many drinks as well.

Chris's manhood has been challenged and his ego

has been crushed in the face of everyone at the

table. He's furious now.

He stands up from the table. Kerry looks up at him and then disregards him. She tries to continue on drinking her glass of wine.

CHRIS

So you just gone disrespect me like that? *(beat)* Huh? *(beat)* Kerry I'm talkn' to you.

She doesn't answer, but instead she ignores him by trying to hold a conversation with Lisa and Lauren.

Brent is still standing where he is, but he knows what's about to go down and he prepares for it.

Mel is looking at Chris because he sees that he's getting frustrated, and he's getting pretty uncomfortable.

Kerry still refuses to answer Chris. So he snaps. He quickly grabs her by the arm. He jerks her out of her seat and says...

CHRIS *(...cont.)*

Woman get yo butt up. I see you smelln' yoself tonight. C'mon let's go to the bathroom and talk.

While Chris is saying this Kerry is arguing back at him. She's so embarrassed, but more scared than anything.

Chris walks her off near the restrooms.

KERRY *(startled)*

Chris what the heck are you doing? Let me go. You crazy and drunk…

Still a wide shot of everybody sitting at the table. When Chris and Kerry walk completely out of frame everyone looks at each other in disbelief and disgust, as if they're startled and surprised at what just happened.

Brent is holding his head down shaking it because he knows what's about to go down, but no one else at the table has a clue. He's seen Chris lose his cool a time or two.

CUT TO:

Cut to mid shot of Dillan.

DILLAN

Whoa!

CUT TO:

Cut to mid shot of Lauren.

LAUREN

What's Chris' problem?

CUT TO:

Cut to wide shot of Brent looking out over the

crowd following Chris and Kerry to see where

they're going with his eyes.

BRENT

That fool done got drunk. He'll be alright in the

morning.

CUT TO:

Cut back to wide shot of everyone sitting at the

table.

LISA

No he *won't* be alright in the morning. He's pretty

pissed. *(beat)* That's what Kerry get for being such

a tramp.

DILLAN

Lisa!? (Beat) Baby don't talk about her like that.

LISA

Whateva. *(beat)* I'm about to go dance. Y'all got too much drama up here for me.

Lisa gets up with her drink in her hand. Dillan tries to follow her to the dance floor. She abruptly stops him in his tracks.

LISA

Ahhhhh, where are you going?

DILLAN

Well I thought you said you wanted to dance?

LISA

Yeah, *I'M* gonna go dance *(beat)* with other people.

Not you. You can stay here. *(beat)* Here, sit down

and have another drink or something.

Lisa pats Dillan on the head like a little boy.

LISA *(...cont.)*

Be right back!

She flees from the table.

Everyone and their mother knows what she's doing

to Dillan, but he hasn't a clue. Dillan drinks his

beer while everyone at the table shakes their head

at him.

Mel starts to look around for Sean and Toni.

MEL

Hey Brent where's Sean and Toni? I ain't seen them all night.

Brent finally takes a seat at the table.
He sits in one of the chairs backwards, and sits his Corona on the table.

BRENT

(he points to the dance floor) They're down there somewhere dancing on the floor. Where you guys should be. *(directing comment towards Lauren)* I'm surprised her behind ain't on the dance floor by now.

LAUREN

Uncle Brent now you know I gotta get my buzz on before I shut it down on the dance floor.

Lauren turns up another shot glass.

Brent starts laughing.

BRENT

Girl you need Jesus.

They all start laughing.

Then Lauren gets up from the table dancing. She tries to grab Mel by the hand, but he doesn't want to go dance. He just wants to sit and drink.

LAUREN

C'mon Mel! Let's go dance.

Mel is almost drunk. He smirks a fake smirk.

MEL

Naw, I'm alright. I'm straight, I'm straight.

Lauren is totally turned off by his response. So she rolls her eyes and goes to the dance floor alone.

LAUREN

Whateva man. You so lame.

Lauren walks off and stumbles down the steps because she is officially drunk for the night. She can't even hold her balance.

Brent and Dillan laugh at her while Mel shakes his

head in embarrassment.

BRENT (laughing)

That fool *gone!*

The guys continue to drink.

SCENE THREE:

(The screen fades into another commercial)

Cut to a skyline view of the people dancing on the dance floor. The music is louder. The lights are really flickering now, and everyone is yelling to the top of their lungs.

Camera pans down to Sean and Toni dancing together. Right next to them is Lisa dancing on some other dude. Moreover, Lauren is dancing on another guy as well.

Sean and Toni realize what Lisa and Lauren are doing and they look at them with a look of disgust.

You see Lauren and Lisa dancing from Toni and

Sean's POV.

TONI

You see these girls? They so bold and out of

control. Where are their husbands?

SEAN

I don't know, but Lauren better stop dancn' on that

fool like that before I have to introduce him to my

fist.

TONI (surprised)

Ahhhh, settle down Uncle Sean. Those girls are

responsible for themselves. Even though you're

their Uncle, you've got to let them live.

SEAN

Man, forget all of that. They're still my girls and as long as I'm around I have to protect them.

Toni turns Sean's head back towad her to refocus him.

TONI

Not before you protect me *(Beat)* and yourself.

SEAN

Man, look at Lisa. Ugh she just don't care. Just disrespecting Dillan.

Toni gets a bit frustrated. She gets tired of dancing and seeing Sean in a frenzy about his nieces. So she stops dancing.

TONI

Ooooo, my feet tired now. (beat) I'm gonna go to the restroom. Meet me back at the table.

SEAN

Ok baby.

Toni begins to walk toward the restroom. Then she turns back around and says...

TONI (sarcastic)

Now don't be playn' around wit none of these chickenheads.

Sean rather brushes her comment off. Gives her a smile. And she smiles back. He heads up to the table. She heads toward the restroom.

The camera follows Toni, from the backside of her, through the crowd into the Ladies' restroom. And when she opens the door she sees Kerry laid out on the floor in a pool of blood, and she's unconscious.

Toni screams.

TONI *(very dramatic)*
OH MY GOD!!! KERRY?!

Toni shuts the door back and screams. She wave towards Brent, Sean, Mel, and Dillan. She's jumping up trying to get their attention. They all see that she's in a panic and they jump over tables and people to run down the stairs toward her.

CUT TO:

Cut to a wide shot of all of them standing in front of the Ladies' restroom door. Toni is frantic right now. She can barely speak.

SEAN *(concerned)*

Toni what's wrong?

TONI *(very frantic)*

My sista! My sista! Somethin' done happened to my sista! Oh Lord!

Dillan and Brent burst through the restroom door, and you see Kerry laying on the floor bleeding and unconscious. You see this from the POV of everyone standing at the door.

102

BRENT *(voice-over)*

Aww shhh--! What in the hell did Chris do?!

You still hear Toni in the background sobbing.

SEAN

Ahhh hell naw! Where that fool go? I'm gone kill

this punk!

Toni rushes to her sister's side on the floor. Still

crying.

TONI *(even more frantic)*

Kerry what happened!? *(beat)* Say something

Kerry! *(beat) (screaming) SOMEBODY GET SOME*

HELP! My sista is bleeding to death!!!

The picture is completely black. Police and ambulance sirens go off.

Toni continues to yell and scream for help between her sobs for her sister. What she really yearns to holler out is that the sister she now holds on the floor—in the pool of blood—is triggering her own trauma. Kerry is a reminder of her own bleeding that no one has taken the time to help her address. As Toni yells help for her sister, she yells for herself too. In addition, the seeming lack of response from the others around them is triggering her even the more.

You may feel just like the women in the restroom floor. You are bleeding with your own issue, yet no one is responding to your call for help or running to your aid. Maybe they *are* responding, but they aren't responding fast enough for you. On the other hand, maybe you're just like Lauren who stands with the men at the restroom door in utter shock of what she sees. She is a *sistah* that has been triggered too. Her own issue of blood now re-activated because of the trauma she sees her fellow sisters grappling with on the floor. She *clearly* sees their issue. However, she responds differently. She weeps for them in silence. It's not that she doesn't care about what they're going through. She's just mute. She can't even find the words or the energy to run to her own fellow sister's side because of her *own* pain that has debilitated her. She stands at the door recollecting on all the times she was laying in a sea of her own issues, yet no one came to her rescue either.

Make no mistake about it. God is the only source of comfort and healing for *all* three women in this scenario. Moreover, He is the source and answer for you. The truth is when women find themselves in the same room with triggered wounds and blood everywhere, the only one to turn to *is* God; the Great Physician. No man, no woman, nothing can help a room full of bleeding sisters like the Lord can. God will help you too as you stand in this room gazing on Toni, Kerry, and Lauren's issues. All you have to do is be willing to *yell*, scream, cry, stand or even sit in your own blood for a moment and acknowledge that you're not ok. It is when you have come to the end of yourself, that you have now come to the beginning of what God can do. There is no one way to respond to your trauma, just as long as you call out to the right source for healing. *Jesus.* For He is the great surgeon who knows how to stop the hemorrhaging. He is the great and mighty healer, with a mighty hand to deliver you and save.

I think it is very important to reiterate here that not all women respond to their issues the same. While one may cry, fight, or go silent, others may act it out in the bedroom, in the boardroom, in the lap of a strip club constituent, or in a random hotel room with a person, she barely knows. In this case; it is not lovemaking or power she is after. She is actually trying to stop the hemorrhaging and anesthetize her pain. Read on to see what I mean.

SCENE FOUR:

INTERIOR: Inside the hospital waiting room. Nighttime around 11:35 PM.

Picture fades into a wide shot scene of Toni, Sean, Brent, and Dillan all standing and sitting in the hospital lobby. They are all worried sick about the wellbeing of Kerry. In addition, Sean and Brent is even more perplexed because they want to kill Chris.

The doctor comes out to speak with them. They all gather around her.

DOCTOR

Well, the good news is Mrs. Locklear did not lose too much blood. She will live. However, the bad news is that she lost enough blood to make her unconscious. Unfortunately causing her to slip into a coma. She is going to be fine though. Now, all we can do is wait until she comes around.

Cut to close up of Toni.

TONI *(crying)*

Well doctor I'm Kerry's sister. Is there any way that I can go back to see her?

Cut to mid shot of doctor. She smiles.

DOCTOR

Sure. You may go back to see her, but for only a little while. In a few, we will be back in to run more tests.

Cut back to wide shot of everyone standing around.

TONI

Thank you so much doctor.

Brent. Dillan, and Sean go back to sit down as Toni walks toward Kerry's room.

Cut to mid shot of Mel and Lauren running through the hospital doors. They run up to where Brent, Dillan, and Sean are sitting.

Cut to wide shot of everyone.

LAUREN

We got here as quickly as we could. The traffic is horrible coming down 20. (beat) Well, what are they saying?

SEAN

She is in a coma.

LAUREN *(surprised)*

Dannnnnng!

Dillan realizes that Lisa isn't with Lauren and Mel.

DILLAN

Wait a minute. Where's Lisa Lauren?

LAUREN

What do you mean where is she? She's not here? I

thought she was with you.

DILLAN

No! Everything happened so fast. I didn't see her at

the club so I assumed she jumped in the car with

you guys.

Everyone looks puzzled that no one can seem to find

Lisa. They all begin to whisper among themselves.

Dillan strays off into the corner to call Lisa.

Cut to wide shot of Dillan over in the corner.

DILLAN *(whisper)*

Hey babe?

Loud music is playing through the phone. It's so loud Dillan can hardly hold the phone to his ears.

DILLAN *(...cont.)*
Hey babe? *(beat)* LISA?! *(beat)* Lisa where are you?

Lisa lets out a sexual scream through the phone. It seems she's having sex with someone. She screams his name out.

LISA *(voice-over)*
Ooooh Mario!

After the scream the phone hangs up.

DILLAN

Hello? HELLO?! *(beat)* What the hell?

Mel and Lauren turn their heads to look at Dillan from behind him, and Brent stands up to see what's going on.

The picture fades to black.

The end credits begin to appear.

TO BE CONTINUED...

(Episode 2 Coming Soon)

HEAL THY WOMAN

THE TREATMENT

WRITTEN BY:
KENYON R. DUDLEY

DIRECTED BY:
GOD

DUDLEY MEDIA GROUP
DUDLEY PUBLISHING HOUSE

PRODUCTION DRAFT: DECEMBER 27, 2013

FULL BLUE DRAFT: MARCH 26, 2021

PREP DATES:
SHOOT DATES:

The Treatment
Heal Thy Woman Backstory

This book series has been fifteen years in the making. Although I was raised in Atlanta, Georgia, I began writing this tale of women while I lived in L.A. during my days of acting. Between auditions, rejection, and loneliness I wrote. I have always been a writer. Being the youngest of eight children and the last one in the house, you learn to live with yourself and your thoughts. I lived with mine by putting them on paper on my bedroom floor. It is how I healed. How I dealt with rejection and pain. How I prayed to God. It was how I reasoned many things that happened in my home and in my life.

Therefore, my L.A. experience was no different; and by far, no coincidence. I met *many* challenges during that time, and I carried the weight of *so* many others' burdens too. So to heal the trauma, I wrote while laying on my bedroom floor. While positioned in my room floor I would often reflect on where my rejection must have stemmed from. I came to realize that most of it came from my mother as she grappled with raising me and my two sisters—at first—as a single mother. For at least the first eight or nine years of my life, I knew her to be a single mother. I knew my mother loved me dearly, and I know that she *still* does. Nevertheless, the truth is I was not always sure how much she actually *liked* me or wanted me around in the earlier years of my life. I would often see her hit the ground running every single day to hustle and make

her living. She was *never* without a job, a side
hustle, or some sort of business going on. In fact,
she and my father ended up owning and operating a
business for twenty-two years before it closed its
doors. She could organize your business like
nobody's business. She was *everybody's*
accountant, lawyer, public defender, prayer warrior,
case manager, and *even* mother. Just about
everyone, especially all of the men in my family
looked to her for guidance on just about everything.
The irony was, she was just as scared as they must
have been back then, but she never would show it.
She always had a good poker face. That is until she
would get home behind closed doors. With her
many private tears, Saturday morning prayers in her
bathroom floor crying out to God for help, her
disagreements behind the master bedroom door with

my father, and the lonely nights she'd wait in bed for him; it was enough for me and my sisters to be the brunt of her frustration and pain at times. Why am I telling you this? It is certainly not to cast my mother in a bad light. I absolutely *love* and adore my mother. I'm her only son that she gave birth to. So we share a deep, special bond. But I realize that my mother is a woman first. And what my mother has had to come through is the very thing that *many* women today are going through. Like so many other women who were fighting to find their identity and happiness in a world of hurt and disappointment, she was drowning many times in a sea of despair; but she knew how to cover it up. She was always one of the best dressed at local events. Her hair was always on point, nails always done, clothes poppin', and everyone just *knew* she had it going on. The truth of the matter was, she did. She had e*verything* another young woman with kids could ever dream of at one time, but she would tell you to this day that her soul was still wounded. I will say that she has made significant strides to finding her own peace and wholeness these days. And I wrote this series to offer a chance at healing or wholeness to other women too.

While living in L.A. I could not help but reflect back on the hurt that I was carrying at the time having much to do with what I had received from her own process. In other words, most of the hurt and pain I felt was not even mine. I was carrying my mother's hurt. I was hurting *with* my mother. I was hurting *for* my mother. Moreover, as I begin to write, I begin to think about *all* of the women out there that were hurting just the same and may be passing on generational trauma and unhappiness to their children because they had not found the proper way to heal. It is not lost on me that some women do not even have children of their own, but they are still rejected and wounded; and instead of passing that toxicity on to children, they pass it on to their boyfriends, their husbands, their friends, their bosses, or whoever is in their pathway at the moment. As I kept writing, I realized that I had a book that spoke to women's pain. I chose to write it in the form of a television script just for kicks! Because a good storyline is always good in a television format, right?!

It is my prayer that you are not only entertained, but also liberated as a woman when reading these pages. This book is for every single mother daring to raise her kids in the face of adversity. It is for every married woman who secretly wishes for a divorce. This book is to every first lady who sits on the front row or up on the stage next to a man who thinks she is invisible. It is for every woman who is grappling with her identity and self-worth after that rape or sexual abuse at the hands of a loved one or a friend. This book is for the woman who was impregnated by her father as a teenager. It is for the woman who chose to sleep with a married man even though she was married to another man. This book is for every woman who has a hole in her soul and she may be seeking to fill it with something that will anesthetize the pain its dark hollowness is causing. This book is for every woman who is ready to tell the truth about her hurt and ready to heal in the same room and scene as other bleeding women. God has called you all to one room. God is after all of you. He arrested me in my apartment room fifteen plus years ago now in Los Angeles, and prompted me to write a love story and a love letter of healing to you. *Hey Woman*, on behalf of God, you have been called, wooed even, into the intoxication of His healing. You *can* heal. I know you do not think so. Some of you may not even want to. You may think that you don't have the time or energy to deal with it. Nevertheless, the mere fact that you were led to this book and series says that it is your time and it is your turn to heal.

Ready, set, Lord, heal thy woman.

Meet
Kenyon R. Dudley

Co-Founder of conglomerates such as DudleyVision Inc., Naomi's Connect Technology LLC, and the Acts Experience Incorporated which houses entities such as the infamous Dudley Publishing House, Dudley Media Group, and The Church of Acts. Kenyon R. Dudley, keeps very busy each day implementing and managing full-scale strategies and operations that will better the local and global community. His goal is effectiveness and leading millions to salvation in Christ.

His experience spans across the borders of Psychology and Mental Health (BA, Mercer University), Ministry, Media and Publishing, Arts and Entertainment, and Business. With over 20 years of ministry experience and 10 years of Corporate America experience, Kenyon R. Dudley brings a wealth of knowledge to every culture and system.

He is the creative brain behind the Acts Experience University (AEU), a virtual university that he and his wife, Jasmine Dudley, founded in 2020. AEU is a library of training content and resources created to equip a generation to live a revival lifestyle as leading church and marketplace ministers of the Gospel. With a hybrid approach, the online university offers a vault of live and pre-recorded courses such as online Master Classes, Life Classes for virtual and in-person discipleship groups, and both online and in-person ministry courses that lead you to become an AEU Graduate and Alumni that is eligible for becoming an AEU Instructor for future courses.

He is the father of 3 biological children, and a riveting modern-day apostolic voice.

Connect with Kenyon R. Dudley

www.kenyondudley.com

Other Notable Works of Kenyon R. Dudley

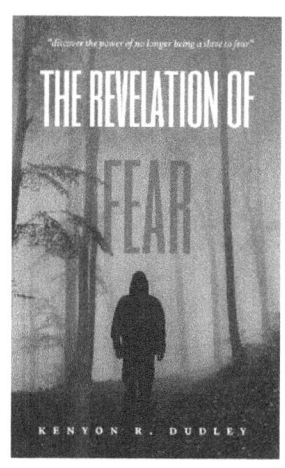